SAY YOU'RE MINE

YOU'RE MINE, 1

JENIKA SNOW

SAY YOU'RE MINE (You're Mine, 1)

By Jenika Snow

www.JenikaSnow.com

Jenika_Snow@Yahoo.com

Copyright © November 2016 by Jenika Snow

First E-book Publication: November 2016

Photographer: Wander Aguiar :: Photography

Cover models: Jacob Hogue & Tiffany Marie

Photo provided by: Wander Book Club

Cover created by: PopKitty

Editors: Kasi Alexander and Lea Ann Schafer

NEWSLETTER

Want to know when Jenika has book related news, and giveaways, and free books?

You can get all of that and more by following the link below!

* * *

Sign Up Here: http://eepurl.com/ce7yS-/

* * *

YOU'RE MINE SERIES

Say You're Mine:
https://amzn.to/2sJ515a

You've Always Been Mine:
https://amzn.to/2JrMAs4

Until Forever:
https://bit.ly/2sHd02R

Say You're Mine

She was mine before I even knew her name...

Felix

When I first saw Maggie, I knew we'd be the best of friends. I wanted that desperately, wanted her in my life, and I'd do anything to make sure that happened.

Until Maggie came in my life I didn't know what love was.

She'll be my first and last.

I'll be her only.

Maggie

I didn't know I could have a friendship like the one I have with Felix. But the friend-zone wall has always been in place. Being too afraid to cross it, I'd rather be in Felix's life than tarnish the relationship we have.

Too much time has passed. I'm done being afraid of the what-ifs. I'm ready to admit how I feel for him, consequences or not.

Felix

Maggie doesn't know the lengths I'll go to keep her in my life, but she will, because the very idea of her with someone else is not something I'll even entertain. She's always been mine, and it's time I step up and show her how much I love her.

My devotion for her goes to the very depths of my soul, and staying back as she lives her life without me by her side is absolutely not an option.

Warning: This story is so sweet it might give you a stomachache, but it will be worth it. It's short, dirty, and featuring a virgin hero and heroine who only love each other. Be prepared to fall in love with this devoted hero who will go to any lengths to make the woman he loves his.

CHAPTER 1

Felix

Six years old

The first time I saw you I knew you were mine.

When she walked into the room, everything around me disappeared. It felt as if was just the two of us.

She was the prettiest girl I'd ever seen, even though her clothes seemed a little too baggy, had stains on them, and holes, too"

Yeah, she was the prettiest girl in the whole world.

I didn't even know her name because the teacher hadn't introduced her to the class yet, but I didn't care.

I knew I wanted to be her friend.

I knew I wanted her to always be near me.

"Class, this is Maggie. She's come all the way to Ohio from Colorado." The teacher touched Maggie's shoulder and smiled at us. "I want you all to make Maggie feel welcome."

I followed Maggie with my gaze as she went to the other side of the room, and finally sat down behind an empty desk. The other kids ignored her, busy working on their paintings.

Her hair was the color of the sun, in two pigtails. I couldn't stop staring at her. I didn't want to. She glanced up at me then, her eyes so big, so blue, they reminded me of the ocean we had just learned about. I hated that she looked sad, that no one was sitting beside her, talking to her.

I had to fix that.

Grabbing my paper and watercolors, I walked over to where she sat. The other kids looked up at me, but I was only focusing on Maggie.

When I sat beside her, I saw her eyes widen even farther.

"Hi," I said, smiling, hoping she wouldn't be scared to be here anymore. "I'm Felix."

She didn't say anything right away and instead looked down at the art supplies I'd brought with me.

I couldn't understand what I felt, but I knew I wanted her to be my friend. I wanted us to be best friends.

"Maggie," she said softly. She looked up then, her blue eyes pretty but still scared.

"Wanna be friends?" I smiled. I hoped she wouldn't laugh at the missing front tooth I had. I'd just lost it and put it under my pillow for the tooth fairy. I'd gotten a whole dollar for it.

She shrugged and looked down at the table again.

"You can think about it, but I'm really nice, and I won't let anyone be mean to you." She looked up again and smiled. It wasn't a big one, but it was a smile just for me. "Hey, you're missing a tooth, too." I pointed to my missing tooth. She stopped smiling, and I felt bad for saying something. "See?" I smiled wider, pointing out the big gap between my teeth. "I lost mine a couple days ago. I got a lot from the tooth fairy." She didn't say anything. "How much did you get?"

She shook her head. "The tooth fairy doesn't come to my house."

"Why not?"

She didn't say anything for a long time. "The tooth fairy doesn't like coming to my house because it's dirty and my mom and dad fight a lot. She's never come to my house, not even when my big brother lost teeth."

I didn't like that at all.

She glanced at me again, and the way she seemed so scared had something inside of me hurting.

I tried to think of what I could do to make her feel better, and then I looked down at the paper and water-colors in front of me.

I grabbed my brush, dipped it in the cup of water the teacher had put on the table, and picked the color I wanted. I knew she watched me. I could feel her eyes on me, and I liked that.

When I was finished, I stared at my picture before handing it to her. Maggie reached out and took it, and for long seconds just stared at it.

"This is for me?" she asked.

I nodded, feeling proud of myself. What I did know was I was keeping Maggie as mine.

* * *

Maggie

HE'D DRAWN a pink heart on the paper. Although it was a little crooked, it was perfect.

He'd made it. Just for me.

I'd never had anyone do anything nice like this for me.

What he wouldn't know was how much a heart on the paper meant to me.

"You and I will be the best of friends," Felix said.

I wanted to be his friend, but I didn't fit in here. My clothes were old, used, and I didn't have nice things like the other girls in the class. Even Felix looked nice, with clothes that didn't have stains on them, or shoes with holes in the side.

"Why would you want to be my friend?" I asked.

He looked at me funny then. "Why wouldn't I want to be your friend?"

I shrugged. "No one ever wants to be my friend." Back at my old school I was called mean things: dirty, poor, ugly. And then Felix reached out and placed his hand over mine. I looked up and stared into his green eyes. They reminded me of grass in the summer.

"I'm gonna be your best friend, Maggie."

I liked how he said my name.

"I'm never letting you go."

And for some reason I really believed him.

CHAPTER 2

Felix

Eighteen years old

I'm keeping you close. I'm keeping you as mine.

I'd known Maggie would be mine since I was six years old. There had never been a time after that when I thought any different. And now, twelve years later, that friendship inside of me had grown strong.

I loved this girl who had changed me so completely, so irrevocably.

For all these years I'd kept her close. It was me and her in this world, and without her I was nothing. Even at eighteen, with graduation only weeks away, I knew this. Hell, I'd known this a long time ago.

She was my best friend, the greatest thing I had in my life, and the very thought of losing her, of something happening that tore us apart, had equal amounts of dread and anger filling me.

But I'd move heaven and earth to make sure I stayed with Maggie, even if that meant turning down college offers so I could go to the same community college as her.

Because nothing in this world mattered if she wasn't by my side.

When we were finally alone at the cafeteria table, I smiled at her. I'd never told her how much I loved her, but surely she could tell? Surely she could see how utterly devoted I was to her? Even if she didn't, none of that mattered. Even if she didn't ever find out that I was hopelessly in love with her, I'd still be by her side.

In this world there was nothing more important than the girl sitting beside me.

* * *

Maggie

Later that evening

FELIX KNEW me better than anyone, but I was afraid to tell him how I truly felt, that I loved him so much.

I didn't feel like I was good enough for him, not with my drunken parents who fought all the time.

Not with my brother who only came home when the girl he was screwing kicked him out.

And not when I had nothing to offer him but the experience of a shitty home life.

You have your whole life to offer him.

"You sure you don't want me to come in?" Felix asked.

He always asked.

I closed my eyes. "I'm sure my parents are screaming at each other, and I don't want you to be subjected to that." *I also don't want you to see how shitty the inside of my home really is, or how my family ignores me, making me feel like I'm nothing but a burden.*

I kept so much of myself from him, the ashamed parts that made me want to scream at how unfair life really was.

But life isn't unfair. I have Felix.

He just stared at me, maybe wanting to fight me on this, to insist we go in together, but after countless times over the years of me saying it was better he didn't go in, he'd stopped pushing me.

"Okay," he finally said. He turned and faced the windshield and ran his hand through his light brown hair. When he looked at me again, I got lost in his green eyes.

God, I loved the color of his eyes.

I loved him.

But he was so smart, had college offers out the ass,

and here I was with one community college offer on the table.

And it was that community college he'd be going to because he didn't want to be away from me.

How did I deserve to have a guy like Felix in my life?

But that college—and the student loan I'd applied for but kept secret from everyone but Felix—was my ticket out of here.

I stared out the window at the front door, not wanting to go yet, but also knowing I needed to because I had work at the diner tonight.

"Hey," Felix said softly. "How about I come over tonight after everyone is asleep?"

I glanced at him, feeling my heart jump a little. It had been a while since he'd come over in the middle of the night and just held me as I slept.

"Okay," I said softly. "That would be really nice." To feel his body close to mine, have his arms wrapped around me, whispering that things didn't always have to be this way.

"I can see how unhappy you are." He reached out and took my hand. "Just a few more months and we can leave." He gave my hand a reassuring squeeze. "The apartment will be ready to go. I've been saving for this, and you don't ever have to think about this place if you don't want to."

He made me so happy I could cry, but I wouldn't, not here, not when my parents' screaming could be heard.

9

"I'm the lucky one." He smiled. "Everything will work out because I'll make sure it does." He gave my hand another squeeze.

I nodded. He was right. Everything would be okay. I'd make sure it was okay for both of us too.

I sat there, wanting to admit how I felt, that I loved him. I wanted him as more than my best friend. He was already the most important person in my life, and it was the fear of losing that, of making things weird, that had me keeping my mouth shut.

"Come here," he said and pulled me in for a hug. I closed my eyes and just let him hold me. "Soon it'll be you and me, only having to worry about school and each other." He pulled back, and we looked at each other.

My heart stopped for a second, and I saw the way he lowered his gaze to my lips.

Kiss me.

Let's forget about everything else aside from this one moment.

I felt his fingers clench gently on my body, and swore he could hear how fast my heart was beating.

And then the screeching of my mother calling my dad a bastard surrounded me in this toxic sensation.

I looked out the passenger-side window and saw my mom throw open the door and stalk out. She waved a bottle in her hand but then stopped and turned toward the house. In a great sweep of her arm, she threw the bottle against the shutters, the glass shattering.

"This isn't going to be your life forever."

I nodded after Felix spoke.

"And you know you are welcome at my house, Maggie."

I faced him. He'd been offering up his house for years, but that actually happening wasn't going to be my reality. I wouldn't put him or his family out.

"You're eighteen now. You don't have to stay here."

I knew that, but I was strong enough to finish out these next few months and leave. Imposing on Felix and his family because my mom and dad fought like cats and dogs wasn't something I wanted to do to them.

This is just the beginning. I'll write my own story soon enough.

* * *

Felix
Let me just hold you.

I QUIETLY SHUT Maggie's bedroom door and crept over to her. I hated creeping around like what I did was wrong.

She was on her side, staring at me, this small smile on her face. I knew her parents were drunks, and I didn't want them catching me in here because I didn't know how crazy they could actually get.

Although judging by the show they gave anyone happening to see them, I knew they wouldn't think twice about tossing a beer bottle at me.

"Hey," I whispered, and she smiled wider and lifted the covers so I could slip inside. Once my shoes were off, I lay down next to her, feeling her body heat seep into me. She smelled sweet, like vanilla cotton candy.

"Hi," she finally whispered back. We were only a few inches from each other, our breathing slow, even.

But my heart was beating hard, fast.

I could have kissed her back in the car.

I could have told her how I felt.

I could have told her what I wanted.

I wrapped my arms around Maggie and pulled her close. She shifted down slightly and rested her head on my chest. We stayed like that for long seconds, and I knew she'd fall asleep.

She always did.

But I loved it, liked that I could watch over her, make sure she was safe while she slept.

"It's all set up," I said softly against her hair. My dad knew a guy that would rent us out an apartment cheap, and so I'd snatched it up, figuring I'd work out any details later. I just wanted to get out of here with Maggie. "I have enough saved up to last us awhile for rent, and I'll work to cover the rest."

"I have money saved up too. It's not much, but I'm helping, Felix."

I ran my hand through her hair. I glanced up at the

wall by the bed, seeing the picture I'd drawn for her all those years ago hanging up, the tape securing it to the wall faded and old. It was a testament to how long she'd had it up there.

That pink heart that meant more today than it ever had before.

"It's old and run-down and not the first place I'd want you to stay in—" I closed my eyes, bringing her even closer.

She pulled back and looked up at me. "As long as I'm with you, I can live anywhere."

That had my heart hurting in the best kind of way.

We wouldn't have much money, but that didn't matter. I didn't care about any of it, because as long as I had Maggie, the world was right.

CHAPTER 3

Felix

One year later

We have the rest of our lives.

I'd been working myself up for so damn long that I was exhausted from it all. Seeing the one person that consumed my thoughts, my heart, my very soul, and not telling her how I felt, took a little piece of me away each day.

I sat in the car, the heater going because it was getting colder, and I wasn't about to freeze my balls off. I stared at Maggie's work, hating that I was this nervous, but feeling alive in the same sense.

I'd thought about that moment in the car last year over and over again, that scene playing through my head like a broken record. But I wanted it on repeat. I wanted it consuming me, taking root and never leaving.

I'd wanted to kiss her so badly, wanted to just give in and press my mouth to hers.

But I hadn't, and I refrained from being anything but her friend.

I wanted that to change.

For the last year a lot had happened.

Graduating from high school.

Moving out of our parents' houses.

Getting settled into this rundown apartment.

Starting college.

Things weren't the way I wanted them, not with where we were living, but that was because Maggie deserved better than what I could probably ever give her.

I was pulled out of my thoughts when I saw the last customer had left. The lights were turned off, and I sat up straighter. I watched Maggie through the window. She didn't even know I was here, waiting for her, so I felt like a real fucking stalker in this moment. But watching her when she didn't know I was, seeing the genuine expressions on her face, the ones not guarded because she was aware of everyone around her, was an honest experience.

She came out, turned to lock the door, and I scanned her surroundings. It was dark, but only seven in the evening. The fucking night crept up like a bastard during these winter months. She turned to face me, but her focus was on her purse as she rummaged through it. I got out, and was about to cross the street to go to her when I heard someone whistle then catcall to her.

"Looking good, sweetheart. Want some company tonight?"

My entire body tensed as the world seemed to go in slow motion in that moment. The guy who was walking toward her had this lewd fucking grin on his face. He inhaled through the cigarette he had between his lips, and exhaled a cloud of smoke in front of him.

I looked at Maggie, could see she was ignoring him, but the panic was on her face. My entire body was tight, my muscles strained. The flight or fight instinct rose up in me.

But it was the fight instinct that won, obviously. No one fucked with Maggie, not without me letting them know exactly the pain they'd feel if they did so.

I didn't hesitate to cross the street and put myself between Maggie at this asshole. I momentarily saw the surprise on her face, probably because she wondered where the hell I'd come from. I knew she wasn't surprised I was defending her.

I'd do that until I took my last breath.

The guy came closer, stopped a few feet from me, and flicked his cigarette butt away.

"What, you trying to protect her from me or something?" The guy chuckled. "I was just admiring a pretty girl." He tried looking around my body at Maggie, but I moved with him.

"You don't fucking look at her," I said in a low, clearly dangerous voice. If he couldn't take the warning I was throwing at him, then he'd find out exactly what I'd do, and the lengths I'd go to protect what was mine.

The guy gave me a "what the fuck" look, and I took a step toward him. He was big, but that might be the oversized jacket he was sporting. Even if this guy had been bigger than me, I still would have gotten rowdy and went to ground for Maggie.

Let it come down to that. Let me show you how far I'll go.

I stared at the asshole, my body ready, my hands curled into fists at my side. I felt Maggie move up behind me, grab my wrist, and gently tug on it.

"Come on, Felix."

I was stone in my place, wanting this prick to make a move so I could beat his ass. But to my disappointment he shook his head and turned to walk away from us. I was tempted to stir the pot and start shit with him, simply because he'd thought it was okay to even speak to her. But I felt Maggie's hand on my wrist, and bit my tongue.

I wanted to get her home. I wanted her to be safe.

"I don't know what you're doing here, but I'm glad you are," she said softly.

I turned and looked at her, wanting to kiss her in that moment. But her cell rang, stopping me from doing anything.

17

She answered the call, putting the phone to her ear. "Hey." A second of silence passed. "It's okay," she said and glanced at me. "Felix is here anyway." After a few moments she hung up. "That was my ride telling me she had something come up and couldn't drive me home."

"Guess it was a good thing I was here." My heart was thundering. I hated the very thought that she could have been out here all alone, that bastard going further than he had.

"Yeah, it really is a good thing you're here. She smiled up at me and my heart thundered even harder.

"Let's get you home." I grabbed her hand and entwined my fingers with hers.

I'd never let her go.

* * *

Maggie

WE SAT ON THE FLOOR, since the shitty couch we had wasn't all that comfortable anyway. On the way home we'd picked up takeout, and half-eaten pasta sat between us.

It wasn't like we had a lot of spending money, but we'd splurged tonight for dinner. I had a feeling it was because Felix had been worried for me and wanted to make me feel better.

Although neither of us was twenty-one and

couldn't buy alcohol, Felix worked with a guy who had given him a six-pack of cheap beer for helping him out. It tasted like warmed piss, but we didn't care.

After the weird night that had gone down even the nasty flavor of this watered down beer tasted good.

"Are you sure you're okay?" he asked again. This had to be the fifth time since we'd gotten home.

"I'm fine, really." I smiled, genuinely okay. "I mean, that guy didn't bother me, not just because you were there, but his words didn't affect me." And they didn't, not really. "Hell, I hear worse than that at work sometimes." I saw the way his jaw tensed, and knew that sentence had pissed him off.

"What?" he said through gritted teeth. "Assholes say shit to you at work?"

I shifted on the floor, uncrossing my legs and shrugging. "I mean, I've had someone ask me to go home with him so he can…" I cleared my throat. "You get the picture." This blast of cold left him and went straight into me. I was staring at the pasta, feeling weird even talking about this. When Felix didn't say anything I glanced up. He looked like he wanted to go hunt down that random guy and bitch slap him.

"You need to tell me when shit like that happens."

I rested my back against the side of the couch. "So what, you can stand guard at my work and give any guy the stink eye if he looks at me the wrong way?" I chuckled, teasing Felix, but sobered when I saw he wasn't smiling.

"Yeah that's exactly what I'd do if I had to." He was dead serious.

I shook my head. "Felix, you can't be by me all the time. Besides, I'm not the first person this stuff happens to, and I won't be the last. Even some of the women I work with talk lewdly about random guys that come in."

He shook his head and looked down. "I'd do anything to make sure you're safe, Maggie."

I heard the sincerity in his words, but I also saw it in his eyes when he looked up at me. "And I'd do the same for you, although you're so big and strong you don't need much protection." I felt my cheeks heat. I couldn't believe I'd just said that. "I mean, that's what friends are for, right?"

Friends.

He was that to me ... and more. I wanted something deeper, something that I'd probably never have with him.

Because I'm too much of a chicken to say anything. Because ruining this already close bond we have scares the ever-loving shit out of me.

He didn't speak for long seconds, just staring at me, something on his mind, clearly. "Yeah, that's what friends are for," he finally said, this weird tone in his voice. When he smiled at me this time I could see it was distant. There was something on his mind, but it was obvious he wasn't going to open up to me about it.

He reached out and pushed a strand of hair behind

my ear, and this tingle settled over me. "Felix?" I said before I could stop myself. He looked into my eyes, and right then and there I wanted to tell him I was *in* love with him. "I love you," I said instead.

"I love you, too." And he pulled me closer and gave me a hug. Being close to him, with his arms wrapped tightly around me, made everything seem okay.

It made everything feel like it would all work out.

CHAPTER 4

Felix

It's time to be honest.

 o more pretending this is what you want.
It had only been a week since picking her up from work and wanting desperately to kick that guy's ass. She was fine, but I knew I'd never get over the possessive feelings I had for her.

I pushed that night, and that asshole, out of my head. It wouldn't do any good to stew over it.

In my eyes she was a queen and deserved to be treated as such. And I'd make sure to keep her safe no matter what. I'd make sure she'd always be protected until I drew my last breath.

I heard the front door open and close, and my heart started beating hard and fast. It always did when she was near, when I knew she was coming home to me.

Coming home ... to me.

She rounded the corner, her focus on whatever she was trying to find in her bag.

"Hey," I said, and she jumped. I grinned.

She looked up at me and smiled. "You scared the shit out of me."

"Sorry," I said, but honestly I kind of liked the surprised look on her face. It was real, genuine. And the smile she gave me afterward, the one that held relief when she saw it was me, made me pretty fucking happy.

"How was your day?" I asked and turned to grab the plate of burgers I'd made for dinner. Our budgets were pretty limited what with us going to school and both of us working between classes. We stretched the money we earned. The savings I had went for rent and utilities, but hell, I had no problem working overtime to make sure she didn't eat ramen seven days a week. And I did just that.

I hated that Maggie was working at all. I wanted to take care of her fully, to make sure I was the one providing for her. I wanted her to just focus on school, to not be stressed out. But my girl was headstrong, stubborn at times, and liked doing things herself. I couldn't fault her for the very traits I loved in her.

"It was fine, although I didn't do the greatest on my economics test, and I spilled coffee all over my shirt at work." She grabbed the bottom of her white shirt and pulled it out so I could see the large brown stain. I got a flash of her belly in the process. Her skin was smooth, her stomach flat. The sight of her navel had my blood rushing through my veins faster.

I cupped the back of her head, pulled her in impossibly close, and closed my eyes as I inhaled deeply.

She smells incredible.

She gave me a friendly hug, but all I was thinking about was how her body fit perfectly with mine, and how I wanted to do so much more with her.

And that's all it took for my dick to come alive. Hell, it took less than that, but I'd been too far gone in the feel and smell of her to try and calm myself down.

Shit.

I didn't want to be one of *those* guys, the ones who couldn't control themselves when they saw a pretty girl. And although I couldn't really help my body's reaction to Maggie, I also wanted to be respectful.

But this wasn't just about seeing a pretty girl. This was Maggie, the one girl I loved so much it physically hurt. Despite the fact being near her brought out this reaction in me. It always had.

"How was your day?" she asked, her voice innocent, sweet.

Fuck, my dick was getting harder by the second.

She had her body pressed right to mine, her breasts to my chest, her softness to my hardness ... in more ways than one.

It wasn't like I didn't hug her or hold her. I did plenty of times, cherished every moment of it, but when I did feel my body start to react, I backed up from the situation. Hell, even holding her while she slept back at her parents' house had been difficult.

Freaking her out with an erection pressed to her belly wasn't exactly what I wanted to do to her.

But then I felt her freeze, felt her lean body go tight against mine at the same moment she came in contact with my raging hard-on.

Fuck.

I should have pulled away right then and there, made up some excuse. Maybe she'd felt me popping wood before? Maybe she'd felt my arousal all these years when I held her, but she'd never said anything?

Maggie pulled away slightly, yet she still had her arms locked around my neck, still had her chest pressed to mine.

I didn't move.

She didn't move.

Hell, I don't even think we breathed.

I'd done so well all these years in keeping myself in check around her, not wanting to put this weirdness between us by admitting my emotions. If she suspected anything, she never let on. Or maybe I was so blinded by my love for her I wouldn't have been able to tell if she had known something.

I pulled back, scrubbed a hand over my head, and felt this weird sensation move over me. She still stared at me, and although there was no judgment, no awkwardness coming from her, I still felt like the air in the room heated uncomfortably.

"I think I'm going to head to bed," I finally said, and just as I turned to leave, she grabbed my arm. Scenarios about her wanting to "comfort" me, wanting to tell me everything was fine, played through my head. I didn't know why I felt so strange right now, but the raging hard-on I was sporting had yet to subside. Hell, just thinking about being pressed against her, smelling the sweet scent that surrounded her, and holding her, had me so needy I couldn't think straight.

I just needed to leave before I made an idiot out of myself.

"I made dinner."

"You won't eat with me?" She sounded a little shocked, and I felt like an asshole for waning to head to my room. But turning around and showing her my pants were still tented, and trying to explain what I was doing about all of this, about how I was now going to explain my emotions to her, weighed heavily on me. There was no getting around this, and I wouldn't lie to her, but right now I needed to think about hot to fix this and move forward.

I needed to think about what to say to her and how to explain that all these years I'd been in love with her.

CHAPTER 5

Maggie

I had wanted to go to Felix right away, but this weird vibe was coming off him.

Maybe he felt awkward that I'd clearly felt his erection?

Maybe he was embarrassed because of it?

Maybe he was ashamed of it?

I knew enough. It wasn't like he could really help his body reacting. But another part of me wanted to feel warm and fuzzy that Felix obviously desired me.

I had my body pressed right to his. Maybe it was just a natural reaction, something he couldn't help?

I tried thinking back on the past when he'd held me. It's not like I'd ever felt anything from him like that, but now that I thought about it, aside from when he held me while I slept, he'd always ended the hugs and moved away from me. Could he have been trying to hide his arousal?

My heart beat wildly in my chest. I was overanalyzing all of this. I needed to tell Felix it wasn't a big deal—although it was, but in the best kind of way. I knew he loved me, and I loved him.

But I was *in* love with him, and just because he got an erection while I hugged him, and just because I knew he cared for me, that didn't mean he felt that same intensity that I did.

I ran my hand over the foggy mirror, the bathroom steamy from the shower I'd just taken. I stared at my blurry reflection, my hair already starting to curl slightly from the humidity. I hated that he'd been so uncomfortable about what had happened he hadn't eaten dinner with me … the incredible dinner he'd prepared. But I wasn't about to just let this slide. I wasn't about to ignore this because he didn't want to talk about it. Even if he was embarrassed and the love he had for me wasn't on the same level as the love I had for him, I needed him to know things were fine.

I shut off the light and headed down the hallway. His room was across from mine, the last door on the left. Although we'd "lucked out" and there were two rooms in this place, I wouldn't have minded sleeping in the same bed as Felix. It wasn't because I wanted to be close to him in the most physical sense, although I definitely wanted that too. It was also because he was my best friend, and I felt safe and secure in his arms.

Standing on the other side of his door, I was tempted to just be bold and open it, let him know things wouldn't change and he'd need to get past the fact things wouldn't change. But that wasn't me, and if I was going to tell him how I felt, which I was contemplating doing, I wanted to be gentle with this.

I ran my hands over the lounge pants I'd put on. The air seemed especially chilled right now, and I felt my nipples harden under the plain white T-shirt I wore. I was nervous, although I tried to tell myself that there was no need to be. This was Felix, and whatever happened, things would be fine … right?

I'm making something into nothing.

I lifted my hand and knocked twice. A second passed before I finally heard him.

"Yeah, come in."

I pushed the door open and saw him sitting on his bed, his back to me, his upper body nude. I could see he still wore his jeans, and my heart beat faster. I stared at the tattoos he had on his arms. He'd had them before we moved, mainly having friends of friends who made deals in exchange for his ink if Felix didn't have the money for them. There had been plenty of times he'd had to work on cars to repay for the tattoos, but I knew to him it had all been worth it.

It didn't matter if he was covered from head to toe with them or didn't have any ink on his flesh.

I'd love him no matter what.

But it also just so happened that I really enjoyed

looking at him with the lines and shapes and the story he had written on his hard, muscular form.

"I wanted to make sure you were okay." I swallowed, my throat dry, my heart beating fast. I didn't know if this situation was the right time to just come clean. It could make things a hell of a lot worse, and far more uncomfortable if Felix didn't reciprocate my feelings.

"I'm fine," he said softly, his back still to me. I was so nervous. I knew telling him I loved him, and that I wanted him to desire me just as much, might drive this wedge between us.

I'm afraid.

He rose from the bed, ran a hand over his hair, and after several seconds he finally turned and faced me. I saw the way his body tightened, watched the play of muscle under his skin. He lowered his gaze down my body, and I felt like he was actually touching me. I knew my nipples were hard, could feel them poking through the material of my too-thin shirt.

"You're probably pretty freaked out about ..." He cleared his throat.

"I think you're more freaked out about it than I am." We didn't move, didn't say anything else for long seconds. I hated this weird silence. We'd never been like this before. "This seems so silly," I finally said, playing this off like it didn't affect me.

But it does.

"But it's not, Maggie." He paused a second, staring

right in my eyes. "It's pretty fucking serious, to be honest."

I knitted my brows and shook my head. "So you were hard." I shrugged, although a flush stole over me. "I'm sure it happens all the time. It's natural."

He smirked, but it didn't look like he was amused.

"I mean, I hate how that one thing has made this awkward now. It shouldn't be like that with us." I took a step closer. "I'm sure if I was a guy, I would have popped a boner, too." I tried for a little humor, but Felix looked serious.

And then he started moving toward me, and the expression on his face had my throat tightening. He stopped when he was only a few feet from me, his big body making me feel even more feminine. Having him so close had me so heated I couldn't even breathe.

"I want us to be the way we were, Felix." I swallowed the lump in my throat. My words came out tight, and I wondered if he could tell how aroused I was.

He shook his head. "I don't want us to go back to the way things were."

"I don't understand," I whispered, although if I was being honest with myself, I hoped he meant exactly what I wanted.

* * *

Felix

Just say you love me back.

I'D WAITED my whole life for this moment, for the balls to come clean about how I really felt for Maggie. I could have done this a long time ago, just been a man and told her the truth, said to hell with any repercussions that might have come from it.

But I'd rather have Maggie as a friend than nothing at all.

Then why am I saying anything right now? Why risk it?

Because I was sick of having to hold myself back, of pretending there wasn't anything more than a close bond of friendship. It was eating me up inside, and having Maggie feel my arousal for her in all its hard glory was just the kick in the ass I needed, I guess.

She stared at me, looking so damn gorgeous, so damn innocent. She made it seem like my boner pressed to her belly hadn't affected her. But it had. I know it had. I just didn't know if it leaned more toward the bad or good side of it all.

"You look … conflicted," she said, and I could see how nervous she was. I didn't blame her. She was probably freaked out by all of this.

You sure you want to do this?

Yeah, I needed to.

"I don't want us to go back to the way things were," I said again. I watched the emotion play across her face. "I love you."

She smiled at me, this sweet, beautiful smile that lit up the whole fucking room. "I love you, too."

"I'm *in* love with you, have been for as long as I can remember."

I felt the air change in the room, sensed it get hot, then cold, over and over again. I tried to gauge her emotions, what she might be thinking by the expressions on her face, but what came out the strongest was shock.

I took another step closer to her. "I love you so damn much, Maggie." I stopped when I was only a foot from her. I inhaled deeply. She smelled so good. "And no matter how much I try and push it down, no matter how much I try and keep this on a friend level—" I shook my head. "I can't. I can't pretend I'm good with being just your friend." I reached out and cupped her cheek. I was pleased she didn't move away. "And as much as I want you in my life and will take you however you will have me, I have to be true and honest with myself." I looked right in her eyes. "But above all else I need to be true and honest to you." I was trying to remain calm, to act collected. I didn't know how she'd react once this really settled in.

The silence stretched on, and I couldn't grasp if it was a good kind of silence. She looked down, and I wanted desperately to know what she was thinking.

"Maggie, talk to me," I finally said. My throat felt tight, my heart racing. "I know this is probably confusing you, maybe even scaring you, but I can't keep it in anymore." She lifted her head and looked at me then. The quiet that came from her had my heart jumping to my throat. "And what you felt downstairs —" I swallowed hard. "I don't want you to think I'm some fucking typical guy that can't control himself." I tried to feign calm. "But the fact is whenever you're near, whenever you say anything, hell, whenever I think about you, my body just reacts."

"Felix." She said my name softly, moving a step closer. We were now just inches apart. She put her hand right on my chest, over my heart, and I knew how strongly she could feel it beating.

It beat for her. It always had, and it always would.

"What is it, baby?" I couldn't stop myself from saying the endearment.

I wanted to know what she thought … desperately.

"Felix, I am so in love with you."

And just like that the world stopped, my heart stalled in my chest, and fuck, the damn planets aligned.

CHAPTER 6

Maggie

"Say it again," Felix said.

I couldn't believe this was happening, but it was, and I didn't want to let this situation between us pass. I didn't want this experience to be just an "in the moment" thing. I wanted this to be the realest thing I'd ever experienced ... that we'd ever experienced.

"I love you, Felix." I swallowed, needing to be strong. "I am in love with you, have been for years."

He closed his eyes and rested his forehead on mine. For long seconds neither of us said anything. Then he pulled me close and just held me.

"You have no idea what it does to me to hear you say that." His words were right by my ear, whispered low, heated.

I felt his erection pressed against my belly, and this intense heat filled me. I grew wet between my legs, my entire body lighting up for Felix. He ran a hand over my back, up and down, slow and easy. But that gentle touch did something wicked to me, had me wanting things I'd only ever dreamed of with Felix.

I knew where this was headed, and I wasn't going to try and rationalize that this might ruin things between us. I wouldn't allow myself to be afraid of it anymore, of being with the only person who looked at me like I was worth something important.

"I love you, Felix," I said again and heard him groan.

"You'll never know how good it feels, how perfect and right this all is to me."

"I know exactly how it feels." I pulled back and looked into his face.

I saw the way Felix looked at my mouth, could feel his need for me, and it was in that moment that I realized so many years had passed where we could have been together.

"It's always been you for me, Maggie. Never was there a time when I questioned how I felt, or thought this wasn't what I wanted." He stroked my cheek with his thumb. "You're the only one I love, the only one I'll ever love."

When he lifted his gaze to my eyes, my heart jumped into my throat. I didn't know what to say in that moment. In my head I screamed out for him to kiss me, to hold me, and to tell me he loved me over and over again.

"You understand what I'm saying, Maggie?" He moved his thumb along my skin in slow, gentle sweeps. "I've been in love with you since before I even knew what that was. I was in love with you before I even knew your name, before you even said one word." The smile he gave me was sweet, genuine. Just for me. "I knew that you were it for me even at that young age."

I felt tears prick at the corners of my eyes.

"I didn't want to say anything and ruin what we had. I guess I needed a kick in the ass to express what needed said." He kissed the center of my forehead. "I didn't want to screw up what we have." He leaned in close again, and I closed my eyes. The scent of him was purely male and slightly spicy.

"To know you're mine, that you want me, too..." His big body shuddered.

"I didn't want to say anything either," I admitted.

This is really happening.

"And even if you hadn't said those three words to me, Maggie, I still would have stayed by your side." He added the slightest pressure to my face, maybe showing me that he was right here with me.

My heart was in my throat. I lifted my hands and gripped his biceps. His flesh was warm, smooth, and I curled my fingers gently into his skin. Felix had always been so strong and had always looked out for me.

"What we have, what we share, that's as real as

anything else in this world." He was now eye level with me. "You're the realist thing in my life, and I won't let you go."

He wanted me the way I wanted him, and I was done waiting, done trying to pretend I could live without him in the way I desperately needed.

"Be with me," I whispered.

I felt him playing with the hair by my ear, and chills raced up my spine. I'd anticipated this, was excited for the possibilities. I also felt like I'd just fallen down this black hole with no chance of finding the bottom.

But I was okay with that.

"For me, it'll only ever be you, Maggie."

He looked at my mouth again, and I felt the tips of his fingers brush along the side of my neck. Every part of me was on fire. I parted my mouth and sucked in a breath.

He moved impossibly closer, but I wanted him pressed right up against me, so there was no denying we were here and about to do this.

Are we about to do this?

I should have felt slightly embarrassed by the sound that left me. It was needy but also filled with pleasure.

And his cock … I couldn't even breathe. He was so big, so hard.

And it's all for me, because of me.

CHAPTER 7

Felix

Only with you can reality be this good.

To say I felt like I was dreaming was an understatement. Not only did my girl love me the way I loved her, but I could feel what was about to happen. I could sense her arousal for me, her need for me.

"Can I kiss you?" I whispered.

"You don't ever have to ask."

I groaned aloud, her words spearing me deep.

I looked at her pink, full lips and wanted to get lost in the sensation of our mouths pressed together. I wanted to kiss her so she couldn't breathe, so she was gasping for air, clutching at me for stability.

I wanted to kiss her so she truly knew what it meant to be ravished by the man who loved her.

Hell, I wanted to be so lost in her I didn't even remember my name.

From the moment I saw her, it had only been her for me.

"We can go as slow or fast as you want." I lifted my hand and cupped the side of her neck, pulling her head slightly toward mine. We were just an inch apart, sharing the same air, the sweet scent that saturated her filling my head.

"How about we start with you kissing me?" Her voice was low, heated.

I didn't stop myself then. I tilted my head, and slanted my mouth on hers. A groan was ripped from me instantly. She was so perfect, so soft … so mine.

Maggie loved me.

The one girl I would die for wanted *me*.

The way she gasped against my mouth and let me have my way with her had me so fucking turned on. I had no doubts I'd come in my jeans like a damn teenager.

"Hold on to me, baby," I couldn't stop myself from saying.

She lifted her arms, wound them around my neck, and rose on her toes so she was totally flush with me. There was no spot on her I wouldn't eventually touch.

My cock jerked behind my jeans, and I wanted more.

I needed more from her.

The rope in me started to unravel, and knew if I didn't grapple with my control, I could lose it and ruin this. I didn't want to go too fast, didn't want to be too rough with my passion.

I wanted to make sure she felt good, that she was right here with me.

She dug her nails into the flesh at my back, and my entire body grew tighter, hotter.

"I need you so bad," I said and found myself walking her backward, toward the bed.

I tangled my hands around her hair, tugging at the strands.

"Don't stop," Maggie gasped against my mouth.

I groaned again. "I have no fucking plans to."

I thrust my tongue into her mouth, this guttural sound leaving me. I used my other hand to span her back, keeping her close.

I stroked my tongue along hers and pulled it deeper into my mouth. She moaned for me. I found myself pressing my dick against her belly, the softness of her stomach against the rock hardness of my dick making my balls draw up tightly.

"You have no idea how much I want you right now." I pulled back and looked into her pleasure-filled face.

"Probably about as much as I want you?"

My heart jackknifed in my chest.

"I want you to be my first and only, Maggie." I wasn't ashamed or embarrassed in the slightest to admit I'd never had sex. I'd saved myself for this girl, for the chance to show her with my body what she meant to me. No other girl had ever compared to her, never even crossed my mind. Maggie was it from the very beginning.

I was possessive of her, obsessed with her, and there was nothing in this world I wouldn't do for her.

"Let me show you how special you are to me." I stared into her eyes.

"I want you to be my first, too, Felix."

I breathed out harshly.

"I'll be your only." I claimed her mouth again, kissed her, and stroked her tongue with mine. "I can't stand the thought of you with anyone but me."

"I don't want anyone but you," she said against my mouth. "It's only ever been you."

I closed my eyes and groaned.

I crushed her to me again, speared my hands in her hair, and kissed her until we were both gasping for air. I had my hands on the sides of her neck, holding her still as I mouth fucked her.

That was the best term I could come up with for the possession I took of her mouth.

She arched into me, her breasts pressing into my chest, letting me feel how hard her nipples were. Damn, I wanted her naked, wanted her bare chest right up against mine. My cock jerked again like a moth-erfucker.

I forced myself to pull back and break the kiss. I

didn't want to, but then again this moment needed done right. If I didn't get some control this would be over before it even started.

Maggie deserved better than that.

Burying my face in her neck, I inhaled deeply, getting intoxicated from the way she smelled.

"Take me to bed," she whispered.

We were right by the mattress, so it was easy enough brining her down onto it. I covered her body with mine, wanting the clothes she wore gone. I pulled back and braced my hands by her head. My forearms were straight so my upper body was off hers and our chests were no longer touching. All I did was stare at her.

She was perfect.

And mine.

"I want to go slow with you, to make this last, but I don't know if I can, baby."

Maggie rose up, and before I could comprehend what she was doing, she had her top lifted and pulled over her head. And then I was staring at her breasts.

"Come closer to me," Maggie said softly.

I'd walk over burning coals if I knew it would make her day.

I'd cut off my own arm if it meant she was safe.

I'd do whatever it took to make sure this woman always looked at me with love in her eyes.

"I want you as close to me as possible, Felix."

I was on her a second later. "Shit, baby." I rested my

forehead on her chest, hearing her heart beating right below the surface of her skin, feeling her warmth spread to me.

"We should probably get fully undressed, right?" There was this teasing heat in her voice.

I held in my groan. I wanted to be so deep in her there wasn't any place on her body … in her body that I wasn't claiming as mine.

I shifted and went for the button of my jeans. Once that was undone and my zipper was pulled down, I stopped. "You're sure about this?"

She nodded instantly. "I've never been more sure about anything in my life." She worked off her bottoms and panties, and I shifted on the bed to take off my jeans and briefs. Then we were both naked, my gaze roaming over her, and Maggie's gaze locked on me.

I was frozen in place as I stared at the creamy, perfect flesh that covered her from head to toe.

I knew there was no way I could make this last, at least not on my end. I was so far gone it was taking all my self-control not to get off right now.

I looked between her legs at her pink, wet pussy. The thatch of hair she had covering her mound was trimmed, dark blonde, and I could see her engorged clit slightly protruding.

For me.

Because of me.

I lifted my gaze over her flat belly, along the indentation of her navel, and stopped when I got to her pert, handful-sized breasts.

Everything about her is perfection.

"I need you," she said, and I groaned.

"Oh shit, baby." I didn't want to make her wait, and I sure as hell didn't want to wait either. We both needed this so badly.

Christ.

"I'll never get enough," I admitted freely. There was no shame in how I felt, in what I desired with this girl.

"Be with me, Felix. Love me."

My throat tightened, my emotions threatening to spill over.

"I need to go slow and easy, make love to you—"

"I want you to lose control. I need you to be authentic, to not try and restrain yourself." She breathed hard and fast. "Because right now that's how I feel, Felix."

Well shit, I could have fallen to my knees right then at her admission. I wanted this moment to be special and so damn memorable, but I was so far gone for her. Never in my life had I felt like losing control, had I felt like I couldn't handle what was about to happen.

But with Maggie all I could think about was unleashing the passion I'd had for her for all these years in the most physical of senses.

And thank God she was right there with me.

CHAPTER 8

Maggie

"*Y*ou're so beautiful," Felix said to me, his voice deep, slightly gruff.

I looked at his body, all hard muscles, golden flesh, and tattoos that made me weak in the knees.

I could have said the same thing to him, but I felt silly calling him beautiful. He was more than that. He was rough around the edges, yet smooth enough he could have been called a pretty boy. He was in shape without obsessively trying to be.

And what he sported down below …

I swallowed hard, this sudden lump in my throat. His dick was huge, long and thick, the crown slightly wider than the shaft.

"You're staring at me like you can't get enough," he

said, his voice even more guttural than just a few seconds ago.

"I don't think I ever will," I admitted honestly.

"Shit, baby."

My heart raced in my chest. Then he grabbed his cock, his hand large but not dwarfing in the slightest what was between his thighs.

Every part of me felt hot, then cold, this wave of emotions and sensations crashing through me. And the way he looked at me ... like he *couldn't* get enough, like he'd never get enough, had a flush stealing over me.

I couldn't think straight, but then again I didn't need to do anything but feel right now.

We were going to do this, really going to finally be with each other, and I knew this would forever change me. This would forever change our relationship.

"I want you so bad." Felix let go of his huge erection and moved closer to me. I smelled his rich, intoxicating scent, and I let it roll over me.

"I think we've waited long enough." Yeah, I said it, meant it. I was so ready for this. I lifted my hands and ran them up his arms, feeling his muscles under the inked-up skin bunch. "I've never been ready for anything more than I am with you." I was wet, so soaked it felt slippery between my thighs.

And it was all because of Felix.

It was all for him.

He made this low sound deep in his chest, part

47

man, part feral animal. Our breathing increased, and I knew without a doubt this would rock me to my core.

In only the best of ways.

Then he was on me, his big body covering mine, his hands on my chest, his mouth on mine. He kissed me for long seconds, plunging his tongue in and out of my mouth, claiming me, making me his in all ways. My legs were spread wide for him, and I felt his cock right on my pussy. He was hot and hard.

"Oh yeah, Maggie," he groaned against my mouth. "I can feel how wet you are for me." He licked my bottom lip, and I couldn't hold in the groan that spilled from me.

He moved his lips over my jaw and started sucking at my pulse point right below my ear, running his tongue along my flesh, gently biting me until goose bumps formed on my entire body. Felix shifted, and his cock slid between my folds. I felt him tense, and we both gasped.

"You're burning up for me."

"I am," I said honestly. "I need you."

He started pressing his erection against my pussy for long seconds while he went back to work with his mouth on mine.

"I want to make you feel good." His voice was so husky and deep.

"You already are." I wasn't going to lie.

"Do you want me to make you feel even better?" he

asked right by my mouth, his lips barely touching mine, his breath warm and spicy like cinnamon.

I was beyond turned on I couldn't even think straight, let alone answer. But I found myself nodding, this involuntary sound leaving me after the fact.

My hands were shaking, but I felt bold, infused with his passion as well as mine. I felt sweat start to form at my temples and the valley between my breasts.

Felix lowered his gaze to my breasts, and I wondered if he took notice at how hard I was breathing, if he could hear it.

"You're sweating." He still stared at my chest, and I lowered mine to see what he was staring at. Beads of sweat were already formed, and before I could say anything or even move, Felix was speaking again.

"I want to lick them off, Maggie." He looked at me then. "Would you let me do that, baby?" He leaned forward slightly, his upper body pressing me farther back on the bed. "Would you like to feel my tongue on you, lapping up that salty water, the evidence of how worked up you are for me?"

A shiver worked its way through my entire body. Who knew hearing Felix say he wanted to lick at my flesh, gathering the sweat from my body, could be such a turn-on?

I heard my heart thundering in my ears, felt it in my throat.

I nodded, telling him without words what I wanted.

His gaze was locked with mine. Then I felt his

tongue on me. I closed my eyes and fell fully back on the bed. I gathered the sheets in my hands, pulled at them, feeling everything in me come alive even more. Felix licked a path between my breasts, his breathing harsh, the noises coming from him guttural.

"Even your sweat tastes sweet, baby."

I opened my mouth and sucked in air, feeling light-headed. But he didn't stop there. He continued to lick my flesh, the arch of my neck, the curve of my breasts, and lower still. He ran his tongue over my belly, dipped it into my belly button, and gripped my waist with his big hands, holding me down, making me take this erotic abuse.

But I wanted more. I wanted so much more.

And when I felt his mouth right over my pussy, his hot breath coming in hard, fast pants, I curled my toes. I could have gotten off right then and there, but I was exerting a lot of control right now.

"Do you want my mouth on you, Maggie baby?"

I felt the vibrations of his voice right on my clit.

"Yes, Felix." I reached up and tangled my hands in his hair. He was licking at my slit, dragging his tongue right up my center, then latching his mouth over my clit. I cried out as the orgasm that rocked through me stole every ounce of my sanity. I couldn't think, couldn't even breathe. I pulled at his hair, keeping him against me, needing his mouth right there.

Even as my orgasm rocked through me, he moved his mouth down my cleft to my opening. There he plunged his tongue in, spreading my pussy lips with his thumbs, and fucked me with his lips and tongue.

"I'll never get enough. Never." He moved back up my body, wrapped his hand loosely around my throat, and kissed me hard and possessively. I tasted myself on him, a sweet, musky flavor that had my heat renewing, had me wanting him right here and now.

At this rate I didn't think I'd be able to walk straight tomorrow, but what a thing to look forward to.

CHAPTER 9

Felix

I'll make the world kneel at your feet.

I wasn't even inside of her yet, and already I was trying not to get off. My balls were drawn up to my body, and I was having one hell of a time keeping myself in control.

"I could come right now, Maggie," I said honestly. I wanted this to last so badly. I wanted to feel her pussy clenching around my cock, milking me because she wanted my cum filling her up. She made the hottest sound.

It was one of need ... of wanting me.

"I'm ready for you, Felix. I need you."

I couldn't stop from moaning at those words. I ran my tongue along her bottom lip, wanting to mouth fuck her desperately. I was tense, my muscles straining under my skin. My cock was so hard, and I felt pre-cum at the tip. Looking down at her face showed me she was right there at the edge. Her cheeks were this gorgeous pink color, and her pupils were dilated. And her lips … fuck, her lips were red and swollen from my kisses.

I wanted her to know she was all mine.

Hell, I wanted everyone to know, and to realize what we had was set in stone.

"I'm not ashamed to admit I'm possessive of you, Maggie," I said as I looked in her eyes. "In fact, I'm proud of that fact. I love knowing that I'd go to the ends of hell if it meant I could keep you forever."

She started breathing harder, and I slid my hand between us and ran my finger along her slit. "Because as barbaric as it seems, I own you like you own me." I grabbed my cock, aligned it with her pussy hole, and stilled.

Her pussy was hot and soaking for me.

"Even though you're not in me yet," she said breathlessly, "you feel so good."

I groaned at hearing her words.

I plunged my tongue inside her mouth, forcing her to take it all.

I was done waiting.

I needed my cock in her pussy now.

"Maggie, baby," I groaned against her mouth, my hips having a mind of their own and wanting to plunge forward, burying my cock inside of her tight, virgin heat. "Baby, I need to be inside of you." She ran her tongue along my lip, and my whole body shivered in response. "Spread wide for me."

"You want me wide?" She was tempting me.

"So fucking wide for me, baby."

She let out a sweet gust of air, and I knew she was losing control.

With the tip of my cock at her entrance, I didn't want to wait anymore.

"Stop thinking about it and just do it." She arched, pressing her breasts against my chest.

I shoved my hips forward, thrusting my cock deep into her. She cried out in pain, and I cursed myself for not having control and going slow.

"No, I'm okay. Don't stop."

Her pussy was so tight, so wet. She was so hot, so primed for me, I almost came right then.

"*Felix,*" she groaned out, her head thrown back, her lips parted.

"Are you okay? I didn't hurt you too much?"

She shook her head, her eyes still closed, her chest rising and falling rapidly. "No. I'm fine. Just don't stop."

"I'll never stop, because you're mine." I was fully inside her now, my balls pressed right up against her ass, her pussy clenching around my cock. "Hold me, dig your nails in me, make me hurt, too."

And she did just that.

I hissed out, loving the sting of pain.

"I need you to move. I need you to make love to me, to fuck me."

"Damn, baby girl. You can't say that to me or I'll come right now." I started moving in and out of her slowly, gently. My pleasure built. The need to stay calm, to make sure this was good for her, was hard to grasp.

I hunched my shoulders forward, lowered my head, and claimed her mouth as I thrust in and out of her.

My dick was so damn hard it ached.

"Does it freak you out to know I want to fill you with my seed? Does it scare you that I want to make you smell like me, be marked by me?" I thrust especially hard in her. She gasped and held on tighter, digging her nails in deeper.

"No." She stared in my eyes. "It turns me on."

"Shit, you feel so good." The feeling of her pussy squeezing my cock, and of her wanting this so damn badly, made me higher than a kite.

"God, Felix," she breathed out.

"Just me, baby."

"That's all I want."

"I want to be so deep inside of you nothing else matters but the two of us."

"Nothing else does matter, Felix."

I smiled at her. She was so right about that.

CHAPTER 10

Maggie

*T*here was pain.

But the pleasure overrode anything else.

"Stay right here with me, baby," Felix said in a deep voice, the strain on his face clear, the pleasure surrounding him.

"I'm right here."

He thrust in slow and easy, and I swore he was holding his breath.

Heat started to build inside of me, that discomfort still there but not as powerful as it had initially been.

He was big and thick, hitting parts of me that had my toes curling and my heart racing.

"You feel so good." He closed his eyes and groaned softly, and that sound had my pulse beating right in my clit. "Touch me, Maggie," he said and opened his eyes.

"Grip on to me as I make love to you." He leaned closer to my mouth. "As I fuck you."

A shiver worked through me.

I had my hands on his biceps, my nails in his flesh. I wanted him as close as he could get. He started pulling out of me; then right when the tip was lodged in my body, he pushed back in, slow and easy, gentle and sweet.

"You don't have to be so gentle, Felix." He stilled, and I knew I'd shocked him. He'd thrust in deeply, had a few hard plunges in me, but I felt like he was holding back. I knew he was trying to sweet with me. "But slow and easy is good, too." I smiled. "I just want you to be with me the way you want."

He buried his face in the crook of my neck again, and I wrapped my arms around him. "You have me, all of me, until the end of time."

He started moving at a steady pace then, and as the seconds moved by and the intensity of my pleasure rose, I just let myself feel.

A spark of pleasure slammed into me, and I couldn't hold in my moan.

"That good, baby?" he asked against my ear, his voice breathless.

"So good, Felix."

He thrust in and out of me slowly and turned his head so he could press his mouth on mine.

This feeling of being filled, stretched, and

consumed was so monumental my eyes roll back in my head.

He was hard where I was soft.

He was masculinity where I was femininity.

My inner muscles clenched around him, and he pushed in deep and hard.

He felt so good on me ... in me.

Felix retreated an inch. The bulbous head of his cock was poised at my entrance. While holding my gaze with his, he thrust in deep and hard once more. I shifted up on the bed, crying out in the process. He was almost all the way out again, then pushed back into me.

Over and over he did this, faster and a little harder with each movement.

I went to close my eyes, but this noise from the back of his throat stopped me.

"Watch me. Look into my eyes as I take you, Maggie." He leaned in and kissed me again. "I love you so much." He kissed me again and again. "You're my life."

He sank back into me. Felix rose up, braced his hands by my head, his forearms straight, and looked down the length of our bodies. He watched as he plunged his cock into my pussy. I swore I heard this growl leave him.

"It's so damn hot watching my cock go into you." His head was still downcast, but he lifted just his eyes to look at me. "And seeing that cherry blood all over my cock..." He shivered. "It's the hottest thing,

Maggie." He went back to watching what was happening between out bodies ... of where he was buried.

He did this for long, pleasurable moments. But then he made this low sound in the back of his throat, gripped my waist, and flipped me over. He covered my back with his chest. It was only a second before I felt him reach between us and place his dick right back in my pussy.

With my head to the side, his body pressed to mine, and the feeling of his hips moving back and forth against me, I felt myself start to rise to the surface of another orgasm.

"That's it," he whispered. "You're so hot and wet, and so slick for me." He started pushing in and pulling out of me faster, harder. "You're mine." He moved my hair away from my face and licked the shell of my ear.

The scent of sex and sweat filled the room. The sounds of our heavy breathing surrounded us. The passion between us was intense, so tangible I felt it lick at my skin like a thousand hands touching me.

The sound of his cock in me, of him fucking me, consumed every part of my being. It was this erotic, auditory pleasure-filled sensation. He only kept me on my belly for a few moments before he flipped me on my back again. I liked the way he was taking control, moving me around the way he wanted me to be.

It was hot.

I stared at Felix, watching the play of his muscles

bunch and flex under his skin, and couldn't stop myself from running my hands over his massive, impressive form.

"Tell me you'll come for me again, baby?" Felix gritted out.

I nodded first, not thinking I could find my voice. Closing my eyes and breathing out harshly, I wanted him to know where I was right now. "Yeah, I am going to come again." And I was, so hard, so fiercely I knew it would rival my first one.

"Yeah, baby?"

I nodded, gasping at the same time.

"Then come for me, get off all over my dick. Milk me, baby."

And just like that, I did.

My pussy muscles clenched around him, and he grunted in response, his hips slamming hard against mine.

"Oh shit, Maggie." He closed his eyes, his jaw clenched tightly. "Here I come."

I forced myself to keep my eyes open. I wanted to see him get off because of *me*.

He groaned harshly again, bucking against me, emptying himself in my body.

"I love you so much." He thrust in deep.

I wanted him as high as I was.

"So. Fucking. Good." Hearing his words, and feeling his body on me, *in* me, had me climaxing again. It wasn't as intense as the last ones, but it was mind and body controlling.

"You're so perfect." His eyes were still closed, but the ecstasy was clear on his face.

My inner muscles clamped down hard, and we both moaned.

"You'll always be mine, and I'll always be yours," he seemed to say to himself. "Oh shit, Maggie. That's *so* it. Squeeze my dick, work for my cum."

His filthy words were an instant accelerant in me.

With his huge body over mine, I felt every hard muscle in him tense further as he reached his peak.

"Yes," I whispered. He was buried deep in me, filling me, making me his. After long seconds Felix finally relaxed atop me, his huge, muscular form dwarfing mine, but making me feel so warm and safe.

We were both sweaty, our breathing erratic, identical. All I wanted to do was stay like this, to just be in our own bubble where nothing would touch us.

"I'm probably crushing you, baby." Before I could protest, Felix rolled off me but kept me right up against him.

"I love you so much," he whispered against my ear.

I smiled and closed my eyes, nothing else mattering except this moment. I could have stayed like this forever.

There wasn't a place on me that didn't want his touch, his smell ... his everything.

"I'll never get enough," he whispered at the crown of my head.

I pulled back and looked up at him. He was already staring at me. The smile he gave me had everything feeling like it was perfectly aligned, like everything we'd been through, or would go through, would be worth it all.

It has *been worth it all.*

"No one will ever compare to you, Maggie. No one." Felix shifted on the bed and cupped the side of my face. He pulled me in close, and I couldn't deny I loved being held by him. I loved everything about him. He made me feel open and alive, made me feel like there were so many possibilities in this world. "I want you as mine, always, Maggie. As my wife, my partner in this life, and the mother of my children."

My heart totally stalled at his words.

"Soul mate is too tame of a word for what I feel toward you."

I lifted my hand and cupped his beard-covered cheek. He'd been slowly growing it out, and I couldn't deny that I loved it. It made me feel especially feminine. "And you're mine." I felt the love he had for me.

"To have you in my life..." He closed his eyes and shook his head slightly. "That's all I've ever wanted."

"I want that, too, all of it, Felix." He crushed me to him, and I loved it. I loved the feeling of being breathless. I loved the way his big body cocooned mine, making me feel so small, so protected.

It was just a shame it had taken us so long to get here. But we were here now, and that was all that mattered.

Life was far too short to not go after what you wanted.

CHAPTER 11

Maggie

Felix wrapped his arm around me and pulled me more firmly back against him. The movie we were watching was a couple of years old, the volume down too low for us to really hear what was going on, but I didn't care. Just being in his arms was good enough for me.

It always had been, and it always would be.

To be Felix's was something I'd wanted in every way since the moment I knew what wanting that even meant. But I'd been too afraid, and I'd come to realize so had he.

I stared at the top of the TV, the pink heart he'd drawn all those years ago proudly displayed in a frame. It was old, the edges frayed, worn. It wasn't as vibrant in color as it used to be, but to me it was the most important, valuable possession I owned.

I'd stared at that picture every night since he gave it to me when we were six. It had been my lifeline when I'd felt like things were falling apart. Even after all these years, I still stared at that drawing and knew everything would be okay.

I didn't need my family in my life, and it was clear they didn't need me either. That situation was behind me, and Felix and I were moving forward.

But now we really had each other in all ways, and I felt like this was exactly where my life was supposed to be. We might not have a lot of money or live in the nicest place, but we had each other, and that's what mattered.

One day we'd have everything we both deserved. We'd have the degrees we were working hard to get, we'd have our own place we could call home, but most importantly we'd always be by each other's side. There was no other option for us in that regard.

"What are you thinking about, baby?" Felix asked in a sleepy voice. I shifted so I could face him now. The couch we were on was small, barely fitting Felix's big body, but we'd made it work between the two of us.

He had his hand on my lower back, his huge palm spread out along my exposed flesh where my shirt rode up. He used his stretch to make sure I didn't fall off the edge, but I also knew he held me because he loved me.

I could see it in his eyes every time he looked at me.

The feeling of his body heat seeped into me, and I moved my hand between us to rest on his bared chest. He wore a pair of sweats, his very male, very muscular bod on display. To say I got tired of seeing him this way, of tracing my fingers over the multiple tattoos he had and the new ones he kept getting, would be an outright lie.

"What's on your mind, sweetheart?" he asked softly and shifted slightly so he could cup my face with his other hand.

"I was just thinking about how much I love you."

He made this deep sound in his throat, tipped my head back, and devoured my mouth with his. We stayed like that for long minutes, our tongues moving together, our breathing mingling as one, and the heat in the room intensifying. When he pulled away, I sucked in a deep breath. I felt how ready he was for me, his erection pressed to my belly, hard, long, thick.

But he didn't make a move to have sex with me, much to my disappointment.

Instead he just stared at me, the love on his face so tangible there wasn't a doubt in my mind he would go to any lengths for me.

The same lengths I'd go for him.

"You're my soul mate," he finally said. "I'd do anything for you, because seeing you happy, seeing that smile on your face just for me, makes anything and everything worth it."

This man had a way of saying things that made my heart flutter.

"And even though all I want to do is marry you right now, make you mine in all senses of the word, I know there is a lot going on in our lives." He lifted my hand and brought it to his mouth. He kissed each finger while staring into my eyes. "But just know this: you are mine forever. I'm not going anywhere, baby."

He pulled me in close, and I pressed my body flush with his. "Good, because you're stuck with me." The sound of his chuckle was deep and vibrated against my ear. Being with Felix made everything okay.

It always had, and I knew it always would.

* * *

Felix

Just say you'll be mine.

"YOU NEED ANYTHING?" she asked from the kitchen.

"Just you," I replied.

She chuckled, but I knew she liked hearing me say these things just as much as I liked telling her them.

Maggie came into the living room, walked by me, and I reached out and pulled her onto my lap. She made the sweetest little sound.

I held her tighter, pulling her back toward me,

wanting to shelter her. We sat there for long seconds, this comforting, serene atmosphere surrounding us. At least it was for me. I sensed she was growing a little distant.

She was quiet, and I knew then she was thinking about her family. She always got like this when she thought about them.

Since graduating and moving out, her family hadn't tried to keep in contact with her. And even though she spent holidays with my family and they loved her like their own, my girl hated that her family was the way they were.

I shifted so we were lying on the couch. I reached for her hand and took it in mine, rubbing my thumb along her flesh.

"Are you thinking about your family?" I finally asked, even though I already knew.

She was silent for a second before answering. "Unfortunately, I am."

For long seconds I just held her, stroking my hand along her arm, feeling the goose bumps form along her body.

"You don't need them in your life if they make you question how you feel about yourself." I took her hand in mine.

"They haven't even tried contacting me once, Felix."

I kissed the top of her head. "I know, baby, and I'm so damn sorry about that."

She shifted even more so I could look into her face. I kept my hand at the small of her back, keeping her close to me, wanting her that way always. "I'll be here for you no matter what, and I'll never let you down."

The smile she gave me lit up the damn room. "I know. And I'll be here for you, Felix." She sighed softly. "I wish sometimes things were different. But to be honest, it isn't about not seeing them or talking with them that bothers me. It's the fact that if I didn't have you in my life, I'd be truly alone."

I cupped the back of her head, keeping her to my chest so she was resting right over my heart. "You feel that?" After a second she nodded. "It beats for *you*. Only you. And I'm not going anywhere. This world means nothing without you in my life, by my side."

"I feel the same way, Felix."

I knew she did, and it made me the luckiest man in the world.

I adjusted so she pulled back and looked up at me.

"Marry me." This certainly wasn't the way I'd wanted to go, or how I saw myself proposing to her. Hell, I could have done this years ago if this was the route I'd planned on taking. But what was the point of waiting? We might not be wealthy, or live lavishly in the least. I might not have the money yet to give her the ring she deserved, but we had each other. "I've wanted to marry you for so long it's imprinted on me. It's in my DNA." She didn't speak, and I worried I'd scared her or, hell, freaked her out. "I certainly didn't see this moment going this way, on the couch, with some lame old movie on TV."

She smiled at me, and I felt like a real man because I'd done that, made her feel a little bit of happiness. I cupped her cheek and stared in her eyes. "I'm already the happiest man on this planet because of you, but if you will be my wife, I'll make sure you're always treated like the queen you are."

She started tearing up then, and I worried they might not be happy tears.

"Shit, Maggie, I don't want you to cry."

She shook her head, closed her eyes, and smiled. "They're happy tears."

"I've been saving up for a ring worthy to be on your finger, and even though I'll keep doing that, I had to ask."

She opened her eyes, and before I could say anything else, she was straddling me. She cupped *my* face, and kissed me. "Of course I'll marry you," she said against my mouth, the saltiness of her happy tears making this moment all the more special.

I wrapped my arms around her, pulled her closer so she was lying on my chest, and couldn't help the smile that covered my face. "You'll never be alone." And I meant that with every part of me, with every ounce of love I had for this girl. Where she went, I went. That's how it was, and that's how it always would be.

* * *

Felix

I do

MAGGIE WAS the love of my life. She always had been. She always would be.

She was that one person that could change another human being just by being in their presence.

And she'd always be mine.

And there was nothing on this planet that could keep me from her.

I closed my eyes, willing myself to calm down, and breathed out slowly. This was the day. This was the moment I'd always envisioned.

Nearly two years had passed since I'd proposed to her on the couch. It seemed like a lifetime to get to this one moment in our lives, but it had been one hell of a journey.

And although I would have been happy to go to the courthouse to make this official, Maggie deserved a real wedding.

She deserved it all, and so I'd strive for the rest of my life to make that possible.

I'd saved up, had a custom ring made for Maggie— because I wanted her to have something unique and just as special as she was. I'd worked my ass off saving money, making sure that we were doing better and could follow through with this next step in our lives.

And we were finally here, together, always.

I stared at the woman I loved more than anything else. She was beautiful in her white lace dress, the veil

JENIKA SNOW

covering her face. I lifted the delicate material up and over her head, and the smile she gave me lit up the entire room.

As the officiate spoke to us and the audience—only a handful of our friends and my mother and father—I could only stare at Maggie. I was lost in her eyes, so in love with this girl there wasn't anything I wouldn't do for her. She might not speak with her family anymore, but she had me and mine, and we showed her as much love as possible. I showed her as much as I could, so much so I wondered if it overwhelmed her.

Then it was time for us to repeat the vows and exchange rings, and I felt my heart slam hard against my ribs.

"I do," she said softly, her smile just for me.

I slipped her ring on, squeezed her hand, and breathed out slowly. "Never was there a time where I questioned how I felt for you." I looked into her blue eyes. She seemed surprised, but then again I hadn't told her I'd written my own vows. Bringing her hands to my mouth, I kissed her knuckles gently. "From the moment you stepped into my classroom all those years ago, I knew you were something special, that you'd be mine." A tear started to slide down her cheek, and I brushed it away. "You'll always be the one for me, and each and every day my love for you grows tenfold." She smiled wider this time, another tear tracking down her cheek. "Maggie Elizabeth, you are the only one for me. You always have been, and you always will be." I pulled her into my body, holding her tightly. "I do." I finally said the words, and our guests laughed softly.

"You may now kiss your bride."

Thank God.

I did just that, kissed her until she was breathless, until she was holding on to me for support. I kissed her like she was my world ... because she was.

EPILOGUE

Felix

Several years later

This is the beginning of the rest of our lives.

y wife.
The woman I loved more than anything else.

My entire world.

I'd always known Maggie was my fate … my soul mate.

I pulled her close, and inhaled deeply. She fit perfectly against me. We'd just made love, and all I wanted to do was be with her again. It wasn't because I was some horny bastard, but because I wanted to show her with my body that I was hers the same as she was mine.

I smoothed my hand down her arm, slipped my fingers through hers, and lifted her hand. I stared at the ring. It wasn't the biggest, and even though she deserved the biggest fucking rock, I'd picked this one out especially for her—had it custom made, too.

Everything I did was for her.

Several years we'd been married now, and it was everything I'd ever thought it would be ... and more. We were both working stable jobs, using the degrees we'd earned, and even had a small house we'd purchased together. We had the room, were financially stable, and I was ready to take the next step with the woman I loved.

I anticipated what our future held.

I could hear her breath become even, slow, and knew she was falling asleep, but I also wanted to talk to her about something that had been on my mind for a while.

"Maggie?" I said softly.

"Hmmm?" she said back in a sleepy voice.

I slid my hand over to her belly and spanned the flat surface with my palm. For a second all I did was feel her stomach moving up and down gently as she breathed. "How would you feel if I said I wanted to try for a baby?" I said softly and felt her tense. She shifted and turned in my arms, and I immediately cupped the side of her face. "The very thought of creating a baby with you makes me so happy," I whispered. "But I want you to feel like this is the right time, too."

She lifted her hand and placed it over mine, which was still on her cheek. "A baby?" she whispered.

I smiled, the thought making me feel pretty good. "Yeah, a baby." I leaned in and kissed her. Moving my hand away from her face, I slid it down her side, skimmed my fingers along the curve and arch of her waist and hip, and moved it so my hand was on her belly again. "I want my baby growing right here." I added the slightest pressure to her stomach. "I want a little bit of both of us running around."

She rested her head on my chest. "I want that, Felix." She lifted her head and stared at me. "I want us to be a family … to *have* a family."

I grinned, feeling so elated I couldn't even contain it. I rolled on top of her, my cock hard, my body ready for her.

Only her.

She spread her legs, allowing me to settle between them. I felt how wet she was, a combination of her arousal for me and also of my cum. I'd filled her up good, made sure she was soaked in my seed.

"You'll have to stop taking the pill right away," I murmured. I ran my nose up the arch, inhaling that sweet scent that always surrounded her. "You're always so ready for me, so primed," I said softly against her ear. I reached between us, grabbed my cock, and placed it at her entrance. Pulling back, I looked into her face, and after only a second I pushed inside of her. She arched her chest out and moaned.

"Say you're mine," I said and thrust deeply into her. She made the sweetest sound.

"Felix." Maggie moaned my name, and I grunted in response. "I'm yours."

I kissed her then, claiming her mouth, her body, her very soul. She owned every part of me right now to the marrow, and I'd show her that my devotion for her ran just as deep.

This life meant nothing to me without Maggie by my side. I don't know what I did to deserve her, but I was never letting go.

* * *

Felix

And then there were three.

THERE WAS nothing more beautiful than watching my woman feeding our baby. I leaned against the door frame of Abigail's nursery, listening to Maggie hum to our little girl. It had only been a few months since Maggie gave birth to Abi, and I'd never thought I could love someone as much as my wife.

But seeing my daughter being born, knowing she was a little part of both of us, had my love overflowing.

My daughter.

My wife.

My girls.

Maggie finished feeding Abi and put her in the crib. She stared down at our baby girl for a few seconds before leaving. I wrapped my arm around her waist and pulled her to my side. We walked a few steps before I stopped and faced her. For long seconds we didn't say anything. I could look at her forever.

"If I could go back in time to when I first saw you, I would just so I could fall in love with you all over again." I pulled her against me even more, held the back of her head, and stared into her eyes. "If I could marry you again, I would, just so I could hear you say 'I do.'" I heard her breath hitch.

"Even after all this time I still get butterflies in my belly with you." She smiled up at me. "That'll never change, not even when we are gray and old."

I leaned down and kissed her. "I can't wait to wear matching tracksuits with you as we power walk through the mall on Sundays." She laughed, and I couldn't help but follow suit.

"I'm glad you already have it planned out."

Seriousness filled me. "I've had my life planned out since the moment I saw you, and it always involves you by my side." I crushed her to me then, kissed her breathless, and just held her. Needing her right then and there, I lifted her in my arms and carried her to our room. "Baby, I need you, like right the fuck now."

She made the sweetest sound in the back of her throat. "I need to be inside of you."

She breathed out, wrapped her arms around me, and I knew she was already primed for me.

I'd never get enough of her.

She was mine, and always would be.

The End

You've Always Been Mine

USA TODAY BESTSELLING AUTHOR

JENIKA SNOW

YOU'VE ALWAYS BEEN MINE (You're Mine, 2)

By Jenika Snow

www.JenikaSnow.com

Jenika_Snow@Yahoo.com

Copyright © January 2017 by Jenika Snow

First E-book Publication: January 2017

Photographer: Wander Aguiar

Cover models: Jonny James & Tiffany Marie

Photo provided by: Wander Book Club

Editors: Kasi Alexander and Lea Ann Schafer

Cover Creator: Popkitty

You've Always Been Mine

Paige

When Erik left town, I thought my world had ended. Even at the tender age of ten I knew how hard my life would be without him. And as I grow older, as the letters between us became sparse to nonexistent, I can't help but feel like a wall has been built around my heart.

There is only one boy for me, and I know I'll never see him again.

Erik

She was my best friend, the only person I knew I couldn't live without.

But we had to leave each other.

Time went on, we drifted apart, and it always felt like I'd left a piece of myself back with her. But I'm a man now, a wounded Marine, and fate brings me back to the one girl who completes me.

Paige has always been mine, and now it's time to prove that to her.

Warning: Tighten that seat belt because you're about to go on an over-the-top, totally unbelievable ride. Featuring a possessive and devoted hero who saved himself for that one girl, it'll still have that sugary-sweet aftertaste you crave. Don't forget that cold glass of water, because you'll need it for the heat this book—and Erik—is packing.

CHAPTER 1

Erik

Welcome back: Twelve years later

*I*t had been so damn long since I'd been back to this town.

Twelve years.

One hundred forty-four months.

Six hundred twenty-five weeks.

Four thousand three hundred and eighty days.

It seemed like a lifetime ago.

It was a lifetime ago.

But I never stopped thinking about her.

I stared at the sign that greeted us. Blue Springs. The town I'd moved away from all those years ago. I was a different person now, a man. I was a Marine, had seen violence, horror. I had a bad leg to show for it, scars, a memory of what I'd done in my life. My memories held darkness and pain, but it wasn't just about getting injured while fighting that stayed with me, that coated me like this thick second skin.

It was about *who* I'd left behind.

The town held so many memories for me. When I'd first left, as a child, not knowing how to cope, I'd cried myself to sleep so many times.

"Can you believe we're back here after all this time?"

I turned and looked at my mom. I knew she was tired, scared, and pissed most of all. But she put up a good front. She stayed strong, and I knew it was because of me. Even if I was a grown man now and should be taking care of her, still she tried to shelter me. Even though I'd seen war and death, been on the receiving end of it all, still she was a mother.

I knew it was for me.

I reached out and took her hand in mine. "Everything will be fine. I'm here now, he's out of our lives, and we can start over." Well, it was starting over in the place we began, but she knew what I meant, I was sure.

And if I ever saw my father again, I'd kick his ass.

Not only did we uproot our life all those years ago because of his new job, but it was only recently that we found out he'd been banging the office secretary for the last five years.

He threw away his family for a piece of ass, a twenty-something-year-old piece of ass at that.

My mom smiled. I was really proud of her for not

putting up with his bullshit and having the strength to leave. I rubbed my leg absently.

"Is it bothering you?" she asked, and I shook my head.

"No. It's just a habit." When a bomb had gone off, shrapnel had gone straight into my leg. Now I had a scar that ran the length of my thigh to my knee. I told myself things happen for a reason. Although I was no longer on active duty, I'd earned a Purple Heart, and was now home to be with my mom during this shitty time.

She left, and I left with her.

No way in hell would I let her do this alone. Even at twenty-two I knew I had to be there for her. I could finish school in Blue Springs. I'd already applied for the spring semester at the community college, and I'd find work somewhere.

"I hate that we had to leave all those years ago, only to come back and stay with your cousins and aunt."

I shrugged. "It's better than staying there with that asshole." I had my hands on my thighs, wanting to punch him right in his fucking face.

"He's still your father. Don't talk about him like that."

I clenched my teeth but was respectful enough not to say anything else. I could have said a shitload about him. Him fucking that woman explained a lot; why he'd seemed distant, stayed later, was gone on "business meetings" on the weekends. He'd neglected us to get his dick wet.

Yeah, I had no fucking sympathy for that bastard.

Silence stretched on for long minutes, and my thoughts went back to all those years ago, to happier times, to a person that hadn't ever let me down.

Paige Masterson.

She'd been my best friend since kindergarten, and for the next four years we'd been inseparable. Leaving her behind when we moved had been the hardest damn thing I'd ever done. I might have only been a child, but even now I still remembered her. I remembered the sweet smell of her and how she made my heart race.

"It's a shame you lost contact with Paige," my mother finally said, breaking up the silence.

I stared out the passenger side window.

It was a fucking tragedy that we lost contact. But I was back in town now, and I had the rest of my fucking life to make it up to her, to be there for her in all the ways that counted.

I thought back to how it had all gone away, how we'd drifted apart. I should have tried harder, been a better friend.

For a year after we moved I wrote to her every day. And if I was lucky I was able to call her. But back then my parents didn't have a cell phone with unlimited minutes. We didn't have the Internet where I could Skype with Paige. I was at the mercy of letters, a calling card if I was lucky, or my parents being generous and letting me call her long distance.

But seeing her again, actually coming back to Blue Springs back then wasn't an option, not when it was a three-day drive straight through, and I didn't have my license. My parents also couldn't afford a plane ticket.

And by the time I was old enough and had enough money, we'd drifted apart, to my devastation.

So those few phone calls had been my saving grace.

But as the years went on, those letters we wrote back and forth grew less and less. Schoolwork, friends, and the distance put this wedge between us. I hated that it had come to that, loathed that we hadn't tried harder to stay connected. Then I'd gone into the military right out of high school. Four years later and here I was now, coming back, wounded, my heart still beating for one girl.

"Yeah, it's a shame."

It is a fucking tragedy.

But I never forgot about Paige.

I never stopped thinking of her as my best friend, never stopped seeing her as my soul mate.

And coming back to town had this excitement tunneling through me the likes of which I'd never felt.

"Although she won't recognize you," my mom said and started laughing. She glanced at me, eyeing my arms and neck. "You went crazy with the tattoos and working out. I doubt even your cousins will recognize you."

The working out wasn't just for my sanity, but because I had to be strong to be a Marine. Not just in body but in mind, as well.

I stared out the window again, thinking about her, imagining what she'd look like now. We might have sent pictures back and forth as the years passed, but I hadn't seen one of her since we were thirteen years old. Was her dark hair still long and wavy? Did her blue eyes pop with color still? The last time I'd physically seen her had been when I was a devastated ten-year-old, wanting to hold her tight and not let go. I could still hear her voice in my head. How much had she truly changed?

As drastically as me?

God, I want to see her so badly.

Even through the shit storm that was our current situation, I'd anticipated coming to Blue Springs and reconnecting with Paige. I had no doubt it would be like I'd never left. You don't have a friendship like that without knowing that person even a thousand years later.

But the one thing that stuck with me, like a living nightmare of reality, was the possibility that she had someone. Hell, she was twenty-two now, the same age as me. For all I knew she could be married, have children.

The very thought of her with someone else, of having a family without me, made me so damn anxious I shifted on my seat.

No, I wouldn't go there. If it came to it and I found out she did have someone, that she was happy, I'd gladly take her in my life as a friend.

I'd take her any way I could have her.

Are you sure you can just let go like that, though?

Now available:

https://amzn.to/2JrMAs4

YOU'RE MINE SERIES

Say You're Mine:
https://amzn.to/2sJ515a

You've Always Been Mine:
https://amzn.to/2JrMAs4

Until Forever:
https://bit.ly/2sHd02R

Want your very own Real Man? Check out the series
HERE: http://amzn.to/2szRFss

WANT MORE?

Find all of Jenika's dirty, sweet, and everything in-between books here:

http://www.jenikasnow.com/bookshelf

NEWSLETTER

Want to know when Jenika has book related news, and giveaways, and free books?

You can get all of that and more by following the link below!

* * *

Sign Up Here: http://eepurl.com/ce7yS-/

* * *

ABOUT THE AUTHOR

Find Jenika at:

Instagram: Instagram.com/JenikaSnow
Goodreads: http://bit.ly/2FfW7A1
Amazon: http://amzn.to/2E9g3VV
Bookbub: http://bit.ly/2rAfVMm
Newsletter: http://bit.ly/2dkihXD

www.JenikaSnow.com
Jenika_Snow@yahoo.com

96894100R00061

Made in the USA
Columbia, SC
09 June 2018